Disclaimer:

We do not own any rights to the Friends T.V. series, and this book has been written in an unofficial capacity. All questions have been constructed using information acquired solely by watching all 10 seasons of the T.V. series 'Friends', therefore it is written with the highest degree of accuracy. If you believe any of the information to be inaccurate, or you have any other general enquiries, please contact the authors at quizbooksdirect@gmail.com and we will endeavour to make any necessary adjustments.

Introduction:

Almost 16 years since the final episode of friends aired, on May 6th, 2004, and since then, it hasn't quite been our day, our week, our month, or even our year. But we still continue to watch the series over and over, and laugh as hard as we did the first time. We also find ourselves finishing off their sentences, and saying their lines before they've happened, because we know it almost off by heart! Well, I hope I can prove you wrong in that last part, with this quiz book, which has been created by watching every episode from start to finish, once again, and writing questions wherever possible.

Even the biggest fans, who thought, like myself, that they knew every little detail, will likely meet their match with many of these questions!

I hope this book brings hours of entertainment to all who read it!

Good luck, and enjoy!

CONTENTS PAGE

Season 1 Questions

Easy

1. What item was hidden in the lasagne Monica cooked?

2. Who teaches Joey how to smoke?

3. What is Phoebe's sister Ursula's job?

4. What song does Marcel play, that Joey, Chandler and Ross all dance to?

5. Who was the maid of honour at Rachael and Barry's wedding?

6. Does Chandler have any siblings?

7. Who accidentally reveals that Ross is in love with Rachael?

8. What does every friends episode title start with?

9. Name the actor who plays Joey.

10. Name the actor who plays Chandler.

11. NAME THE ACTOR WHO PLAYS ROSS.

12. NAME THE ACTRESS WHO PLAYS MONICA.

13. NAME THE ACTRESS WHO PLAYS RACHAEL.

14. NAME THE ACTRESS WHO PLAYS PHOEBE.

MEDIUM

15. WHO SAYS "YOU CANT CHANGE YOUR PARENTS, BUT BOY IF YOU COULD... I'D WANT YOURS", AND WHO ARE THEY SPEAKING TO?

16. WHAT DID CAROL AND SUSAN WANT THE SECOND NAME OF THE BABY TO BE?

17. WHAT IS THE NAME OF MONICA'S BOYFRIEND WHO ALL OF THE OTHER FRIENDS LOVE, HOWEVER IT IS REVEALED AT THE END OF THE EPISODE THAT HE 'CAN'T STAND THEM'?

18. HOW LONG WERE ROSS AND CAROL MARRIED?

19. WHO DOES CHANDLER GET STUCK IN AN ATM VESTIBULE WITH?

20. WHO SAYS "I FOLD LIKE A CHEAP HOOKER WHO GOT HIT IN THE STOMACH BY A FAT GUY WITH SOARS ON HIS FACE"?

21. WHO SAYS "ONCE THE CARDS ARE DEALT, I'M NOT A NICE GUY"?

22. WHO WON THE MONEY ON THE FINAL HAND IN POKER BETWEEN ROSS AND RACHAEL?

23. WHO GETS SHOT BY A TRANQUILLISER DART?

24. WHAT NAME WAS JOEY GOING TO USE WHEN TRYING TO COME UP WITH A STAGE NAME?

25. WHAT STAGE NAME DID PHOEBE SUGGEST JOEY USE?

26. WHAT DID CHANDLER GIVE RACHAEL FOR HER BIRTHDAY?

27. WHAT DID JOEY GIVE RACHAEL FOR HER BIRTHDAY?

28. WHAT DID ROSS GIVE RACHAEL FOR HER BIRTHDAY?

HARD

29. WHAT DID CAROL AND SUSAN INITIALLY WANT TO NAME THE BABY, IF IT WAS A BOY (FIRST NAME)?

30. WHAT DID CAROL AND SUSAN INITIALLY WANT TO NAME THE BABY, IF IT WAS A GIRL (FIRST NAME)?

31. WHAT WAS THE NAME OF THE GELLER'S FAMILY DOG?

32. WHAT IS THE NAME OF THE CHARACTER JOEY PLAYS WHO IS A SMOKER?

33. WHEN PHOEBE CHECKED HER BANK ACCOUNT THE FIRST TIME, IN "THE ONE WITH THE THUMB", HOW MANY EXTRA DOLLARS WERE IN THERE?

34. WHAT FREE GIFT DOES PHOEBE'S BANK SEND HER AFTER SHE REPORTS AN ERROR?

- WHEN CHANDLER IS TOLD HOW ANNOYING HIS SMOKING IS, WHAT DOES HE SAY IS ANNOYING ABOUT:

35. MONICA:
36. JOEY:
37. ROSS:

38. WHAT DOES JOEY SAY IS ANNOYING ABOUT PHOEBE?

39. WHAT DOES PHOEBE SAY IS ANNOYING ABOUT RACHAEL?

40. HOW MUCH MONEY DID THE SODA COMPANY GIVE PHOEBE BECAUSE OF THE THUMB SHE FOUND IN THE CAN?

- IF PHOEBE WAS OMNIPOTENT FOR A DAY, WHAT 4 THINGS WOULD SHE WANT?

41.
42.
43.
44.

45. WHAT DID CHANDLER SAY HE WOULD DO IF HE WAS OMNIPOTENT FOR A DAY?

46. WHAT DID JOEY SAY HE WOULD DO IF HE WAS OMNIPOTENT FOR A DAY?

47. HOW MANY STEPS ARE THERE FROM JOEY AND CHANDLER'S APARTMENT TO CENTRAL PERK?

48. WHO WAS THE FIRST TO BREAK THE "NO DATES FOR NEW YEARS" PACT, AND WHO WITH?

49. WHO WAS THE SECOND PERSON TO BREAK THE "NO DATES FOR NEW YEARS" PACT, AND WHO WITH?

50. WHO WAS THE 3RD PERSON TO BREAK THE "NO DATES FOR NEW YEARS" PACT, AND WHO WITH?

51. WHAT IS THE NAME OF THE GIRL CHANDLER HAS TO FIRE AT WORK?

52. WHERE WERE RACHAEL AND BARRY GOING TO HAVE THEIR HONEYMOON?

53. WHAT FAKE NAME DOES MONICA GAVE, WHEN SHE MEETS THE GIRL WHO STOLE HER IDENTITY?

54. WHAT WERE JOEY'S GOODBYE WORDS TO MARCEL?

55. WHAT IS THE NAME OF THE BOY MONICA DATES WHO IS A SENIOR IN HIGH SCHOOL?

56. WHAT IS THE NAME OF THE WOMAN JOEY'S DAD IS HAVING AN AFFAIR WITH?

57. WHAT IS THE NAME OF THE SHRINK PHOEBE DATES?

SEASON 1 ANSWERS

EASY

1. RACHAEL'S ENGAGEMENT RING

2.. CHANDLER

3. WAITRESS

4. A WIMBA WAY (IN THE JUNGLE)

5. MINDY

6. NO

7. CHANDLER

8. "THE ONE"

9. MATT LE BLANC

10. MATTHEW PERRY

11. DAVID SCHWIMMER

12. COURTENEY COX

13. JENIFER ANISTON

14. LISA KUDROW

MEDIUM

15. MONICA SPEAKING TO ROSS

16. WILLICK-BUNCH

17. ALAN

18. 7 YEARS

19. JILL GOODACRE

20. JOEY

21. ROSS

22. RACHAEL (HOWEVER ROSS HAD THE BETTER CARDS, BUT DIDN'T SHOW THEM).

23. PHOEBE

24. JOSEPH STALIN

25. FLAME BOY

26. TRAVEL SCRABBLE

27. A BOOK

28. A PIN JUST LIKE HER GRANDMOTHER HAD

HARD

29. MARLIN

30. MINI

31. CHI CHI

32. DAMONE.

33. $500

34. A FOOTBALL PHONE

35. MONICA: HER SNORT WHEN SHE LAUGHS.

36. JOEY: CONSTANT KNUCKLE CRACKING

37. ROSS: OVER-PRONOUNCING EVERY WORD

38. WHEN SHE CHEWS HER HAIR

39. SHE NEVER SERVES THEM WHAT THEY ORDER

40. $7000.

41. WORLD PEACE

42. NO MORE HUNGER

43. GOOD THINGS FOR THE RAINFOREST

44. BIGGER BOOBS

45. MAKE HIMSELF OMNIPOTENT FOREVER

46. PROBABLY KILL HIMSELF

47. 97

48. CHANDLER, HE ASKED JANICE

49. PHOEBE, WITH DAVID THE SCIENTIST

50. MONICA, SHE ASKED FUN BOBBY

51. NINA

52. ARUBA

53. MONANA

54. 'MARCEL I'M HUNGRY'

55. ETHAN

56. RONNIE

57. ROGE (ROGER)

SEASON 2 QUESTIONS

EASY

1. HOW DID ROSS FIND OUT THAT RACHAEL LIKED HIM?

2. WHAT IS THE NAME OF THE CHOCOLATE SUBSTITUTE MONICA IS PAID TO MAKE RECIPES WITH?

3. WHAT IS JOEY AND CHANDLER'S FAVOURITE T.V. SHOW TO WATCH TOGETHER?

4. WHO IS CHANDLER'S FAVOURITE CHARACTER FROM THIS SHOW?

5. WHAT IS THE NAME OF CHANDLER'S NEW ROOMMATE AFTER JOEY LEAVES?

6. HOW IS JOEY'S CHARACTER IN 'DAYS OF OUR LIVES' KILLED OFF?

7. WHEN JOEY AND CHANDLER TRY TO LOOK MORE LIKE RICHARD, WHICH OF THEM GROWS THE MOUSTACHE AND WHICH OF THEM BUYS CIGARS?

8. WHAT IS THE NAME OF PHOEBE'S BROTHER?

9. WHAT IS PHOEBE'S BROTHER'S FAVOURITE HOBBY?

10. WHAT IS RACHAEL'S DAD'S PROFESSION?

11. RACHAEL GETS CHICKEN POX IN THIS SEASON, TRUE OR FALSE?

MEDIUM

12. WHAT WAS MR. HECKLES HOLDING WHEN HE DIED?

13. WHICH THEORY DO ROSS AND PHOEBE HAVE AN ARGUMENT OVER WHETHER IT IS REAL OR NOT?

14. MR HECKLES' WILL SAYS THAT ALL OF HIS POSSESSIONS WILL BE LEFT TO WHO?

15. WHAT BAND DO MONICA, CHANDLER AND ROSS GO TO SEE FOR ROSS' BIRTHDAY?

- NAME 5 OF THE THINGS ROSS WRITES ON HIS LIST ABOUT RACHAEL, WHEN CHOOSING BETWEEN HER AND JULIE:

16.
17.
18.
19.
20.

21. WHAT DID ROSS WRITE ON JULIE'S LIST WHEN DECIDING WHO TO CHOOSE BETWEEN HER AND RACHAEL?

22. WHAT IS THE NAME OF JOEY'S STALKER?

23. WHAT PRESENT DOES JOEY GIVE CHANGER "FOR ALWAYS BEING THERE FOR HIM"?

24. As you are walking into Joey and Chandler's apartment, is Joey's chair on the left or the right?

25. What is Richard Burke's profession?

26&27. What tattoo does Rachael get, and where?

28. Why does Joey get fired from 'Days of Our Lives'?

29. What car does Richard Burke drive?

30. What do the bullies from Central Perk steal from Chandler?

HARD

31. IN WHICH CLOTHES STORE DO JULIE AND MONICA GO SHOPPING?

32. WHAT IS THE NAME OF THE AFTERSHAVE JOEY IS TRYING TO OFFER SAMPLES OF AT THE BEGINNING OF THE SERIES?

33. SOMEONE NEW COMES INTO JOEY'S SECTION TO TRY AND OFFER AFTERSHAVE SAMPLES. WHAT IS THE NAME OF THE AFTERSHAVE THEY ARE OFFERING?

34. WHAT INSTRUMENT DID CHANDLER AND MR HECKLES BOTH PLAY?

35. WHAT IS THE NAME OF THE MAN CHANDLER IMPERSONATES OVER THE PHONE TO GET A DATE?

36. WHAT DOES RACHAEL ORDER FROM THE RESTAURANT ON MONICA'S BIRTHDAY?

37. WHAT IS THE NAME OF THE LAWYER WHO INTRODUCES MONICA, CHANDLER AND ROSS TO THE BAND?

38. MONICA WAS GIVEN WHICH FOOD FROM HER MEAT SUPPLIER AT WORK WHICH LEAD TO HER BEING FIRED?

39. WHAT FRUIT DOES ROSS HAVE AN ALLERGIC REACTION TO?

40. WHAT IS MONICA ALLERGIC TO?

41. WHAT DID ROSS BUY CAROL AND SUSAN FOR CHRISTMAS?

42. WHAT DID ROSS BUY HIS PARENTS FOR CHRISTMAS AS BEN'S PRESENT?

43. WHO BREAKS THE RADIATOR KNOB IN MONICA AND RACHAEL'S APARTMENT?

44. WHAT IS THE NAME OF RACHAEL'S MOTHER?

45. WHAT IS THE NAME OF THE BEER THAT MARCEL FEATURES IN AN ADVERT FOR?

46. HOW MUCH MONEY DOES JOEY GIVE CHANDLER FOR ALL THE MONEY HE HAS LEANT HIM?

47. WHAT NUMBER IS MONICA AND RACHAEL'S APARTMENT?

48. HOW OLD IS MONICA IS SEASON 2?

49&50. WHEN PHOEBE AND RACHAEL DECIDE TO GET TATTOOS, WHICH TATTOO WAS PHOEBE GOING TO GET, AND WHY?

51. WHAT IS THE AGE GAP BETWEEN MONICA AND RICHARD?

52. HOW OLD IS JOEY IN SEASON 2?

53. WHO WINS THE GAME OF FOOSBALL BETWEEN CHANDLER AND JOEY, TO DECIDE WHETHER JOEY WILL TAKE IT TO HIS NEW APARTMENT?

54. WHAT IS THE NAME OF THE EX-GIRLFRIEND OF CHANDLER'S NEW ROOMMATE?

55. WHAT IS THE NEXT AUDITION ESTELLE GETS JOEY, AFTER HE IS FIRED FROM 'DAYS OF OUR LIVES'?

56. WHAT IS THE NAME OF THE BOOK ABOUT FEMALE EMPOWERMENT THAT PHOEBE, RACHAEL, AND MONICA ALL READ?

57. HOW MUCH MONEY DID JOEY SPEND ON THE GLASS PARROT IN HIS NEW APARTMENT?

58. HOW MUCH MONEY DID JOEY SPEND ON THE LARGE MODEL PLASTIC DOG IN HIS NEW APARTMENT?

59. WHO DOES CHANDLER SAY IS "OLDER THAN SOME PEOPLE, BUT YOUNGER THAN SOME BUILDINGS?

60. WHAT IS THE NAME OF THE MAN IN THE NAVY WHO PHOEBE SPENDS 3 DAYS WITH, EVERY 2 YEARS?

61. WHAT CORNER OF THE BED DOES MONICA THINK THE DUVET TAG SHOULD BE?

62. WHAT JOB DOES CHANDLER GET JOEY AT HIS WORKPLACE?

63. WHAT ARE THE NAMES OF JOEY'S FAKE CHILDREN WHEN HE COMES TO WORK WITH CHANDLER?

64. WHAT IS THE NAME OF JOEY'S FAKE WIFE WHEN HE COMES TO WORK WITH CHANDLER?

Season 2 Answers

Easy

1. Rachael drunk called him

2. Mockolate

3. Baywatch

4. Yasmine Bleeth

5. Eddie

6. He falls down an elevator shaft

7. Joey buys cigars and Chandler grows a moustache

8. Frank J.R

9. Melting things

10. Doctor

11. False

Medium

12. A broom

13. Evolution

14. "The noisy girls in the apartment above mine"

15. Hootie and the Blowfish

16. A little spoiled

17. Too into her looks

18. Chubby ankles

19. Just a waitress

20. Kind of ditsy

21. Not Rachael

22 Erika

23. A gold bracelet

24. The right

25. Ophthalmologist (eye doctor)

26&27. A heart, on her hip

28. Because in an interview he said that he writes a lot of his own lines.

29. A Jaguar

30. His hat

HARD

31. BLOOMINGDALES

32. DIJON FOR MEN

33. HOMBRE

34. CLARINET

35. BOB

36. THE SIDE SALAD

37. STEVIE FISHER

38. 5 STEAKS AND AN EGGPLANT

39. KIWI

40. CAT HAIR

41. TWO TOWELS WITH 'HERS' WRITTEN ON BOTH

42. A PICTURE FRAME

43. ROSS

44. SANDRA GREEN

45. MONKEYSHINE

46. $812

47. 20

48. 27

49&50. A LILY, BECAUSE HER MOTHER'S NAME WAS LILY

51. 21 YEARS

52. 28

53. JOEY

54. TILLY

55. CAB DRIVER NUMBER 2

56. 'BE YOUR OWN WIND KEEPER'

57. $1200

58. $200

59. RICHARD BURKE

60. RYAN

61. THE BOTTOM RIGHT CORNER

62. ENTRY LEVEL PROCESSOR

63. ASHLEY AND BRITTNEY

64. KAREN

Season 3 Questions

Easy

1. Who describes themselves as "Hopeless and awkward and desperate for love"?

2. Who is Gunter in love with?

3. Who does the Dutch girl at the Thanksgiving football game say she would rather date, Joey or Chandler?

4. Who gets Rachael an interview at Bloomingdales?

. Which of these catchphrases belongs to which person?
5. "Oh No...."
6. "Could I Be...."
7. "I Know!"

8. Who put a suggestion in the suggestion-box at the restaurant where Monica works, for the staff to use roller-skates?

9&10. Who buys the chick and who buys the duck which live in Joey and Chandler's apartment?

11. What does Rachael convince Ross'

GIRLFRIEND BONNIE TO DO?

MEDIUM

12. ROSS REVEALS TO RACHAEL THAT HE HAD FANTASIES ABOUT WHICH CHARACTER FROM WHICH MOVIE?

13. WHAT FOOD DOES MONICA MAKE TO HELP GET OVER HER BREAK UP WITH RICHARD?

14. WHAT DOES JANICE'S HUSBAND SELL?

15. WHY DOES PHOEBE REFUSE TO GO TO THE DENTIST?

16. WHAT IS THE "GIANT POKING DEVICE" MADE OUT OF?

17. WHAT ARE THE TEAMS IN THE 3V3 FOOTBALL GAME THEY PLAY ON THANKSGIVING (BEFORE THEY CHANGE TEAMS)?

18. WHAT ARE THE NEW TEAMS IN THE 3V3 THANKSGIVING FOOTBALL GAME AFTER THEY SWITCH PLAYERS?

19. WHICH OF JOEY'S SISTERS DID CHANDLER FOOL AROUND WITH?

20. WHO TELLS RACHAEL THAT ROSS CHEATED ON HER?

21. WHICH OF THE GROUP THINKS THEY NEED "A NEW WALK"?

22. WHAT DOES RACHAEL GIVE CHANDLER, TO HELP HIM QUIT SMOKING?

23. PETE BECKER LEAVES A CHEQUE FOR MONICA AS A TIP, FOR HOW MUCH MONEY?

24. WHAT AGE IS FRANK J.R. WHEN HE WANTS TO GET MARRIED TO ALICE?

25. WHO DOES FRANK J.R. ASK TO BE HIS BEST MAN?

26. DOES RACHAEL EVENTUALLY GO ON A DATE WITH MARK?

27. WHAT IS THE NAME OF RACHAEL'S BOSS?

28. TRUE OR FALSE. WHEN THEY ALL GO DOWN TO THE BEACH HOUSE, THEY PLAY STRIP POKER?

HARD

29. WHAT SONG DOES ROSS THINK IS THE MOST ROMANTIC SONG OF ALL TIME?

30. WHAT SONG DOES RACHAEL THINK IS THE MOST ROMANTIC SONG OF ALL TIME?

31. WHAT IS THE NAME OF THE MAN WHO WAS STALKING URSULA?

32. FINISH THE SONG THAT ROSS SUNG AS A CHILD: "I AM BEE, I DRINK TEA..."

- CHANDLER AND JANICE HAD A LIST OF 5 CELEBRITIES THEY ARE ALLOWED TO SLEEP WITH. NAME AS MANY PEOPLE IN CHANDLER'S LIST AS POSSIBLE:

33.
34.
35.
36.
37.

- NAME AS MANY CELEBRITIES AS YOU CAN ON RACHAEL'S LIST OF CELEBRITIES SHE IS ALLOWED TO SLEEP WITH:

38.
39.
40.
41.

42.

- NAME AS MANY CELEBRITIES AS YOU CAN ON ROSS' LIST OF CELEBRITIES HE IS ALLOWED TO SLEEP WITH:

43.
44.
45.
46.
47.

48. WHAT DOES RACHAEL'S DAD EAT WHEN RACHAEL AND ROSS GO OUT TO DINNER WITH HIM?

- WHEN JOEY IS TEACHING STUDENTS TO ACT, ONE OF HIS STUDENTS GETS AN AUDITION FOR THE SAME PART AS HIM.

49. WHAT IS THE NAME OF THE CHARACTER THEY BOTH AUDITION FOR?
50. WHAT IS THE NAME OF THE SHOW?
51. WHAT ADVICE DOES JOEY GIVE HIS STUDENT FOR THE AUDITION?

52. WHAT IS THE NAME OF JANICE'S HUSBAND?

53. HOW MANY BROWNBIRD COOKIES DID ROSS SELL FOR THE GIRL WHO'S LEG HE BROKE (INCLUDING THE ONES HE BOUGHT HIMSELF AT THE LAST MINUTE IN AN ATTEMPT TO WIN)?

54. HOW MANY BOXES DID ROSS SAY THE WINNING BROWNBIRD SOLD (APPROXIMATELY)? A = "OVER 1000",

B = "OVER 1500", C = "OVER 2000"

55&56. WHICH BOOK DOES JOEY HIDE IN THE FREEZER, AND WHICH BOOK DOES RACHAEL INSIST IS MORE SCARY THAN THIS BOOK?

57. WHAT IS THE NAME OF THE GIRL THAT ROSS SLEEPS WITH WHILST HE AND RACHAEL ARE "ON A BREAK"?

58. WHEN RACHAEL ORDERS A PIZZA, WHEN HER AND ROSS ARE FIGHTING, WHICH TOPPING DOES ROSS ASK TO REMOVE, BUT RACHAEL ORDERS EXTRA?

59. AT WHAT AGE DID CHANDLER START SMOKING?

60. WHAT CAUSED CHANDLER TO START SMOKING FOR THE FIRST TIME?

61. WHAT IS THE NAME OF THE AUNT THAT MONICA GOT THE DOLLHOUSE FROM, AFTER SHE DIED?

SEASON 3 ANSWERS

EASY

1. CHANDLER

2. RACHAEL

3. CHANDLER

4. MARK

5. PHOEBE
6. CHANDLER
7. MONICA

8. PHOEBE

9&10. JOEY BUYS THE CHICK, AND CHANDLER BUYS THE DUCK.

11. SHAVE HER HEAD

MEDIUM

12. PRINCESS LEIA FROM STAR WARS

13. JAM

14. MATTRESSES

15. SHE BELIEVES SOMEONE WILL DIE EVERY TIME SHE GOES.

16. CHOPSTICKS

17. JOEY, MONICA AND PHOEBE VS CHANDLER, RACHAEL AND ROSS

18. BOYS VS GIRLS

19. MARY ANGELA

20. GUNTHER

21. JOEY

22. A HYPNOSIS TAPE

23. $20,000

24. 18

25. JOEY

26. YES

27. JOANNA

28. FALSE. THEY PLAY STRIP HAPPY DAYS GAME

HARD

29. TUPELO HONEY

30. THE WAY WE WERE

31. MALCOM

32. WONT YOU DANCE AROUND WITH M.E

33. KIM BASINGER
34. CINDY CRAWFORD
35. HALLE BERRY
36. YASMINE BLEETH
37. JESSICA RABBIT

38. CHRIS O'DONNELL
39. JOHN F. KENNEDY JR
40. DANIEL DAY-LEWIS
41. STING
42. PARKER STEVENSON

43. UMA THURMAN
44. WINONA RYDER
45. ELIZABETH HURLEY
46. MICHELLE PFEIFFER
47. DOROTHY HAMIILL

48. LOBSTER

49. NICK THE BOXER
50. ALL MY CHILDREN
51. TO PLAY THE CHARACTER GAY

52. GARY

53. 872

54. OVER 2000

55. THE SHINING
56. LITTLE WOMEN

57. CHLOE

58. ANCHOVIES

59. 9

60. HIS PARENTS' DIVORCE

61. AUNT SYLVIA

SEASON 4 QUESTIONS

EASY

1. WHAT DOES MONICA GET STUNG BY, AT THE BEGINNING OF THE SEASON?

2. WHO PEED ON MONICA?

3. WHAT NICKNAME DOES PHOEBE HAVE?

4. WHAT IS PHOEBE'S MOST POPULAR SONG?

5. WHO WANTS TO BECOME THE "ULTIMATE FIGHTING CHAMPION"?

6. WHAT INSTRUMENT DID ROSS PLAY IN HIGH SCHOOL AND COLLEGE?

7. WHICH OF THE GROUP ACTUALLY LIKED THE MUSIC ROSS PLAYED?

8. WHICH OF THE GROUP GOES ON A DATE WITH SOMEONE FROM POUGHKEEPSIE?

9. WHO IS "ALWAYS THE HOSTESS"?

10. IN RETURN FOR GETTING BACK THEIR APARTMENT, WHAT DO MONICA AND RACHAEL DO?

11. WHICH OF THE THREE GIRLS DRESS UP IN WEDDING DRESSES?

MEDIUM

12. HOW LONG WAS THE LETTER THAT RACHAEL WROTE TO ROSS?

13. IN RESPONSE TO RACHAEL'S LETTER, DOES ROSS TELL HER "IT DOES" OR "IT DOES NOT"?

14. WHICH OF THE GROUP TELLS PHOEBE THAT HER MOM IS NOT IN A CAT?

15. WHAT DOES MONICA ACCIDENTALLY LOSE IN ONE OF THE QUICHES, WHEN COOKING FOR HER MOTHER'S PARTY?

16. TRUE OR FALSE. PHOEBE HAD TO LIVE ON THE STREETS BEFORE THE AGE OF 16?

17. WHEN ROSS AND MONICA WERE KIDS, HOW DID THEY INSULT EACH OTHER IN FRONT OF THEIR PARENTS WITHOUT THEM KNOWING ("A WAY OF GIVING THE FINGER WITHOUT ACTUALLY GIVING IT")?

18. WHICH OF THE GROUP HAVE KISSED GUNTHER?

19. WHAT GIFT WAS JOEY GOING TO GIVE KATHY FOR HER BIRTHDAY?

20. WHAT IS THE NICKNAME OF ROSS AND CHANDLER'S FRIEND FROM COLLEGE WHO WAS MEANT TO BE COMING TO NEW YORK TO PARTY?

21. TRUE OR FALSE: RACHAEL CAN ONLY EAT TIC TACS IN EVEN NUMBERS.

22. EVERY WEEK, THE TV GUIDE COMES TO CHANDLER AND JOEY'S APARTMENT. WHAT NAME APPEARS ON THE ADDRESS LABEL?

23. IF RACHAEL AND MONICA WIN THE BET TO SEE WHO KNOWS EACH OTHER BETTER, WHAT DO CHANDLER AND JOEY HAVE TO DO?

24. WHAT IS JOEY'S FAVOURITE FOOD?

25. TO ATTEMPT TO BREAK UP WITH JANICE, CHANDLER TELLS HER THAT HE IS BEING TRANSFERRED TO WHICH COUNTRY?

26. WHAT TYPE OF FOOD DID PHOEBE CRAVE WHEN SHE WAS PREGNANT?

27. TO TRY AND IMPRESS JOSHUA, WHAT DOES RACHAEL DRESS UP AS?

- WHAT DO FRANK AND ALICE NAME THEIR 3 BABIES?

28.
29.
30.

31. WHY WAS JACK GELLER UPSET WITH THE BILL FOR ROSS AND EMILY'S WEDDING?

HARD

32. WHO TOOK RACHAEL TO THE PROM IN HIGH SCHOOL?

33. WHAT IS THE NAME OF THE JANITOR OF THE APARTMENT BUILDING?

34. WHAT IS THE DATE OF RACHAEL'S BIRTHDAY?

35. WHAT IS KATHY'S FAVOURITE BOOK, WHICH CHANDLER BUYS FOR HER BIRTHDAY?

36. MONICA BECOMES THE HEAD-CHEF OF A RESTAURANT, WHICH SHE INITIALLY WROTE A TERRIBLE REVIEW FOR, WHIST WORKING AS A FOOD CRITIQUE. WHAT IS THE NAME OF THIS RESTAURANT?

37. HOW MANY OREO'S CAN JOEY FIT IN HIS MOUTH?

- JOEY AND CHANDLER TRY TO GUESS ALL 5 ITEMS IN RACHAEL'S SHOPPING BAG. NAME AS MANY OF THE 5 AS YOU CAN (IN ANY ORDER).

38.
39.
40.
41.
42.

43. WHAT IS MONICA'S BIGGEST PET PEEVE?

44. ACCORDING TO CHANDLER, WHAT PHENOMENON SCARES THE BEJESUS OUT OF HIM?

45. MONICA AND ROSS BOTH HAD A GRANDMOTHER WHO DIED, AND CHANDLER AND JOEY BOTH WENT TO THE FUNERAL. NAME THAT GRANDMOTHER.

46. WHAT IS THE NAME OF CHANDLER'S FATHER'S LAS VEGAS ALL-MALE BURLESQUE?

47. WHAT WAS MONICA'S NICKNAME WHEN SHE WAS A FIELD-HOCKEY GOALIE?

48. RACHAEL CLAIMS WHAT, IS HER FAVOURITE MOVIE?

49. WHAT IS RACHAEL'S ACTUAL FAVOURITE MOVIE?

50. IN WHAT PART OF HER BODY DID MONICA GET A PENCIL STUCK AT AGE 14?

51. MONICA CATEGORISES HER TOWELS. HOW MANY CATEGORIES ARE THERE?

52. JOEY HAD AN IMAGINARY CHILDHOOD FRIEND. WHAT WAS HIS NAME AND PROFESSION?

53. WHAT DOES RACHAEL SAY CHANDLER'S JOB IS?

54. HOW DO JOEY AND CHANDLER GET SEASON TICKETS FOR THE KNICKS?

55. HOW LONG WERE ROSS AND EMILY TOGETHER BEFORE THEY GOT ENGAGED?

SEASON 4 ANSWERS

EASY

1. A JELLYFISH

2. CHANDLER

3. PHEEBS

4. SMELLY CAT

5. PETE BECKER

6. KEYBOARD

7. PHOEBE

8. ROSS

9. MONICA

10. MAKE OUT FOR ONE MINUTE

11. ALL 3 OF THEM

MEDIUM

12. 18 PAGES FRONT AND BACK

13. IT DOES

14. ROSS

15. A FINGERNAIL

16. TRUE, SHE WAS 14 AT THE BEGINNING.

17. BANGING THEIR FISTS AGAINST EACH OTHER

18. PHOEBE

19. A PEN THAT IS ALSO A CLOCK.

20. GANDALF

21. FALSE. MONICA CAN ONLY EAT TIC TACS IN EVEN NUMBERS.

22. MISS CHANANDLER BONG

23. GET RID OF THE CHICK AND THE DUCK

24. SANDWICHES

25. YEMEN

26. MEAT

27. A CHEERLEADER

28. CHANDLER
29 FRANK J.R J.R
30. LESLEY

31. BECAUSE EMILY'S PARENTS TRIED TO TRICK HIM

INTO PAYING FOR THE REMODELLING OF THEIR HOUSE.

HARD

32. CHIP MATHEWS

33. MR. TREEGER

34. MAY 5TH

35. THE VELVETEEN RABBIT

36. ALLESANDRO'S

37. 15

38. APPLES
39. TORTILLA CHIPS
40. YOGURT
41. DIET SODA
42. SCOTCH TAPE

43. ANIMALS DRESSED AS HUMANS

44. MICHAEL FLATLEY, LORD OF THE DANCE

45. ALTHEA

46. VIVA LAS GAYGAS

47. BIG FAT GOALIE

48. DANGEROUS LIAISONS

49. WEEKEND AT BERNIE'S

50. HER EAR

51. 11

52. MAURICE & SPACE COWBOY

53. A TRANSPONSTER

54. THEY WIN THEM IN A "HIGHEST CARD WINS" GAME, AGAINST MONICA AND RACHAEL

55. 6 WEEKS

SEASON 5 QUESTIONS

EASY

1. ON WHAT CONDITION DID EMILY SAY SHE WOULD MOVE TO NEW YORK?

2. WHO WAS THE FIRST OF THE FRIENDS TO FIND OUT ABOUT CHANDLER AND MONICA?

3. ROSS HAS A BET THAT CHANDLER CAN'T GO 1 WEEK WITHOUT DOING WHAT?

4. WHO WAS THE SECOND PERSON TO FIND OUT ABOUT CHANDLER AND MONICA?

5. WHICH OF THE GROUP HAS A 'WORK LAUGH'?

6. WHO WAS THE THIRD PERSON TO FIND OUT ABOUT CHANDLER AND MONICA?

7. WHO DID ROSS' NEW APARTMENT PREVIOUSLY BELONG TO?

8. WHAT DID JOEY FIND FASCINATING ABOUT HIS DEALER ON THE BLACKJACK TABLE IN VEGAS?

9. WHO ATE ROSS' THANKSGIVING LEFTOVER SANDWICH?

10. TRUE OF FALSE. ROSS AND JANICE HAVE SLEPT TOGETHER.

MEDIUM

11. AFTER COMING BACK FROM LONDON, RACHAEL DECIDES THAT PHOEBE WILL MAKE ALL OF THE DECISIONS ABOUT HER LOVE LIFE FOR HER. TRUE OR FALSE?

12. WHY WAS JOEY IN A LOT OF PAIN, WHIST PHOEBE WAS GOING INTO LABOUR?

13. WHAT DID PHOEBE THINK JOEY'S PAIN WAS?

14. WHAT IS THE NAME OF THE "YETI" THAT MONICA AND RACHAEL FOGGED?

15. WHAT NICKNAME WAS CHANDLER GIVEN AT COLLEGE AFTER HIS TOE WAS CUT OFF DURING THANKSGIVING?

16. WHAT WAS JOEY'S COVER STORY FOR CHANDLER AND MONICA, AFTER HE WAS CAUGHT WITH A NAKED PICTURE OF MONICA?

17. WHEN ROSS MOVES INTO HIS NEW APARTMENT, HOW MUCH MONEY WAS HE ASKED TO CHIP IN TO GIVE TO HOWARD THE HANDYMAN, FOR HIS RETIREMENT?

18. WHERE DOES PHOEBE FIND A POLICE OFFICERS BADGE?

19. WHAT IS THE NAME OF THE POLICE OFFICER PHOEBE DATES?

20. DOES BEN GET THE PART FOR THE T.V. COMMERCIAL HE AUDITIONED FOR?

21. JOEY THOUGHT HE HEARD GUNSHOTS WHEN A CAR BACKFIRED, AND HE TRIED TO SAVE ROSS' LIFE. TRUE OR FALSE?

22. WHO BUYS RACHAEL'S SPHINX CAT?

23. WHICH OF THE GROUP HATES HAVING ANYTHING NEAR THEIR EYES?

HARD

24. WHERE WERE ROSS AND EMILY GOING TO HAVE THEIR HONEYMOON?

25 THE DOCTOR WHO DELIVERED PHOEBE'S BABIES, WAS A HUGE FAN OF WHICH FICTIONAL CHARACTER?

26. ON THEIR FIRST WEEKEND AWAY TOGETHER, WHICH CELEBRITY DID CHANDLER AND MONICA SEE WAITING FOR AN ELEVATOR?

27. WHO DOES ROSS SELL ALL OF HIS FURNITURE TO, AFTER EMILY ASKED HIM TO REPLACE ALL HIS FURNITURE?

28. WHEN ROSS AND CHANDLER WERE AT COLLEGE THEY HAD FAKE ID'S. WHAT WAS THE NAME ON ROSS' FAKE ID?

29. WHEN ROSS AND CHANDLER WERE AT COLLEGE THEY HAD FAKE ID'S. WHAT WAS THE NAME ON CHANDLER'S FAKE ID?

30. JOEY TRIES TO WRITE HIS OWN PLAY, HOWEVER HE DOES NOT KEEP UP WITH THE SCHEDULE THAT ROSS GAVE HIM, BECAUSE HE AND CHANDLER WERE PLAYING WHICH GAME?

31. WHAT IS ROSS' NEW YEARS RESOLUTION FOR 1999?

32. WHAT IS PHOEBE'S NEW YEARS RESOLUTION FOR 1999?

33. WHAT IS JOEY'S NEW YEARS RESOLUTION FOR 1999?

34. WHAT IS RACHAEL'S NEW YEARS RESOLUTION FOR 1999?

35. WHAT IS THE NAME OF CHANDLER'S BOSS?

36. ROSS TRIES TO RETURN HIS BROKEN IN HALF COUCH IN EXCHANGE FOR STORE CREDIT. HOW MUCH CREDIT DOES HE RECEIVE?

37. WHAT IS THE NAME OF THE PIZZA DELIVERY GIRL THAT ROSS TRIES TO FLIRT WITH?

38. JOEY'S GRANDMOTHER COMES OVER TO WATCH JOEY IN A NEW EPISODE OF A T.V. PROGRAMME, HOWEVER HIS PART WAS CUT OUT. WHAT IS THE NAME OF THE T.V. PROGRAMME HE WAS CUT FROM?

39. HOW MUCH DID RACHAEL PAY FOR HER SPHINX CAT?

40. WHAT DOES MONICA GIVE CHANDLER, FOR THEIR 1 YEAR ANNIVERSARY?

Season 5 Answers

Easy

1. Ross could not see Rachael anymore

2. Joey

3. Making fun of anyone

4. Rachael

5. Chandler

6. Phoebe

7. Ugly Naked Guy

8. He was his 'identical hand twin'

9. His boss

10. True

Medium

11. False, Monica is correct

12. He had kidney stones

13. Sympathy pains

14. Danny

15. Sir Limps-a-lot

16. That he (Joey) slept with Monica

17. $100

18. Under the couch in Central Perk

19. Gary

20. No

21. False. He was trying to save his meatball sandwich.

22. Gunther

23. Rachael

Hard

24. Athens

25. Fonzie

26. Donald Trump

27. Gunther

28. Clifford Alvarez

29. Roland Cheng

30. Fireball

31. To do

SOMETHING NEW
EVERY DAY

32. TO PILOT A
COMMERCIAL
JET

33. TO LEARN TO
PLAY GUITAR

34. TO GOSSIP
LESS

35. DOUG

36. $4

37. CAITLIN

38. LAW AND
ORDER

39. $1000

40. 2 TICKETS TO
LAS VEGAS

Season 6 Questions

Easy

1. When Ross marries Rachel, how many marriages has he had in total?

2. What problem does Ross have after he whitens his teeth?

3. In "The One That Could Have Been", where there is an alternate reality as all their lives had gone in different ways, what job does Chandler take?

4. What is the name of the student that Ross begins to date?

5. When Joey's fridge breaks, what does he do with the contents?

6. Who helps Chandler pick Monica's engagement ring?

7. Which regular location in the show does Joey take a temporary waitering job at?

8. Which member of the gang do they discover hasn't cried since they were a child?

MEDIUM

9. Where is everyone at the beginning of series 6?

10. What is Joey's agent called?

11. At which university does Ross get a temporary job lecturing?

12. Joey finds the keys to an expensive car. What type of car was it?

13. What is the name of Phoebe's dad?

14. When Rachel is moving out of Monica's apartment, and they are getting emotional, how does Phoebe spark an argument?

15. Name one of Rachel's two sisters.

16. What, does Ross claim, is Unagi?

17. Recount the rhyme that helps Joey remember what day of the week it is.

18. In which episode in series 6 do Chandler and Monica get engaged?

19. Which famous actor is the character Paul Stevens played by?

20. How does Ross refer to how the relationship with Elizabeth should be regarded, given he thinks it is not technically against the rules?

21. What was known as 'The Routine'?

22. When Phoebe and Ross help Joey rehearsing for his part in Mac and C.H.E.E.S.E, what do they discover?

23. What does Joey promise to teach Wayne, the character who controls the robot from Mac and C.H.E.E.S.E, in order to keep his job?

24. When Monica and Chandler agree to give each other homemade Valentine's Day presents, what does Chandler giver her?

HARD

25. WHAT DOES PHOEBE THINK IS UNIQUE ABOUT GETTING MARRIED IN LAS VEGAS?

26. WHAT NUMBER DO MONICA AND CHANDLER DECIDE THEY MUST ROLL ON THE DICE IN THE CASINO AT LAS VEGAS IN ORDER TO GET MARRIED?

27. WHEN MONICA AND CHANDLER ARE GOING TO MOVE IN TOGETHER, WHAT DOES CHANDLER WANT TO DO WITH RACHEL'S OLD ROOM?

28. WHEN CHANDLER IS MOVING IN WITH MONICA, AND WANTS TO GIVE JOEY MONEY WITHOUT HIM FEELING LIKE IT'S 'CHARITY', HOW DOES HE DO THIS?

29. WHAT IS WRONG WITH THE ENGLISH TRIFLE THAT RACHEL MAKES AT THANKSGIVING?

30. WHAT DOES RACHEL AND PHOEBE CLAIM UNAGI IS?

31. WHEN ROSS WOULD TEACH ELIZABETH IN CLASS, WHAT WAS HIS SECRET NICKNAME FOR HER?

32. WHAT WAS PAUL'S (ELIZABETH'S FATHER, WHO IS DATING RACHEL) OLD NICKNAME THAT STILL HAUNTS HIM?

33. WHAT DOES PHOEBE WANT HER TOMBSTONE TO READ?

34. How much does Joey try to charge Chandler for his broken fridge?

35. When Rachel buys an apothecary table from Pottery Barn, and knows that Phoebe won't approve, where does she say she bought it?

36. What does Chandler say when when Ross shows them the joke he got printed in Playboy?

37. Where was Joey's new roommate from?

38. Finish the quote by Chandler. 'Joey's got a really bad hernia, but it's nothing that a little...'

39. What is the name of the character that controls the robot in Joey's show, Mac and C.H.E.E.S.E?

40. What, do they discover, was the reason for the fire at Rachel and Phoebe's apartment?

Season 6 Answers

Easy

1. Three.

2. They're too white.

3. He becomes Joey's assistant.

4. Elizabeth.

5. He eats everything.

6. Phoebe.

7. Central Perk.

8. Chandler.

Medium

9. Las Vegas.

10. Estelle.

11. New York University.

12. A Porsche.

13. Frank Buffet.

14. She gets them to think about all the negative things about each other.

15. Either Amy or Jill.

16. A state of control whereby you're prepared for any danger.

17. Monday, one-day. Tuesday, two-day, Wednesday, when? Huh? What day? Thursday! The third day!

18. The final episode, number 25.

19. Bruce Willis.

20. He says it will be 'frowned upon'.

21. A dance Monica and Ross used to do.

22. That they both believe themselves to be brilliant actors.

23. How to talk to women like he does.

24. A mixtape, that Janice had once given him.

Hard

25. She thinks that if you get married in Las Vegas, you're only married in Las Vegas.

26. An eight.

27. Make it a games room.

28. He bets him money on playing table foosball, and then the made up game 'cups'.

29. She accidentally combines the recipes for trifle and cottage pie.

30. A kind of sushi, freshwater eel.

31. Cutie McPretty.

32. Chicken Boy.

33. 'Phoebe Buffet: Buried Alive'

34. $400.

35. A flea market.

36. 'That is funny. It was also funny when I made it up.'

37. Australia.

38. 'Laser eye surgery won't fix'.

39. Wayne.

40. Rachel's hair straighteners.

SEASON 7 QUESTIONS

EASY

1. WHAT IS THE NAME OF RACHEL'S ASSISTANT?

2. WHAT HOLIDAY DOES ROSS TRY TO TEACH BEN ABOUT DURING CHRISTMAS?

3. TRUE OR FALSE, JOEY IS SCARED OF SPIDERS.

4. WHICH TWO CHARACTERS GET LOCKED OUT ON THE ROOF, AND HAVE TO USE THE FIRE ESCAPE TO GET DOWN?

5. WHO DOES JOEY TAKE WITH HIM TO THE AWARD CEREMONY FOR HIS NOMINATION FOR AN ACTING AWARD?

6. ONE OF ROSS' STUDENTS ASKS HIM TO CHANGE HIS GRADE FROM A FAIL. WHAT REASON DOES HE GIVE FOR ASKING FOR THIS?

7. WHO IS JOEY'S NAP PARTNER?

8. HOW DOES RACHEL MEET TAG?

9. WHY DOES PHOEBE BUY JOEY A SPIDER, AND A DRUM KIT?

10. HOW DOES JOEY REFER TO HIS ADAM'S APPLE?

MEDIUM

11. WHAT DO ROSS AND RACHEL DO TO STEAL MONICA'S THUNDER WHEN HER AND CHANDLER GET ENGAGED?

12. WHICH CHARACTER'S GRANDMOTHER HAD A SECRET COOKIE RECIPE?

13. WHEN CHANDLER, MONICA, AND ROSS ALL REVEAL EACH OTHER'S SECRETS, WHAT IS THE SECRET ABOUT CHANDLER ?

14.. WHAT DOES ROSS DRESS UP AS AT CHRISTMAS/ HANUKKAH, TO TRY TO MAKE BEN EXCITED?

15. CHANDLER AND RACHEL SPEND AN EPISODE EATING SOMETHING THAT WAS MEANT TO BE DELIVERED TO SOMEONE THAT LIVES DOWNSTAIRS. WHAT WAS IT?

16. WHO DOES PHOEBE HAVE PLANS WITH ON THE NIGHT THAT DAVID COMES BACK FROM MINSK?

17. THE GANG INCORRECTLY SAY THAT MINSK IS IN RUSSIA, WHERE IS IT ACTUALLY?

18. WHAT DOES PHOEBE DO WITH THE FIRE ALARM THAT WON'T STOP BEEPING?

19. RACHEL CLAIMS SHE LEFT SOME PAPERS ON TAG'S

DESK, BUT TAG SAYS THEY WERE NEVER PUT THERE. WHO WAS RIGHT?

20. ROSS WANTS TO PLAY THE BAGPIPES AT MONICA AND CHANDLER'S WEDDING. WHY IS THIS?

21. HOW DOES CHANDLER RESPOND TO PHOEBE AFTER THIS DIALOGUE, TALKING ABOUT THE WEDDING PREPARATION?
MONICA: 'YOU JUST STICK TO YOUR JOB'
PHOEBE: 'WHAT IS YOUR JOB?'

22. WHAT IS THE NAME OF THE GIRL THAT JOEY AND ROSS BOTH MEET AS SHE MOVES INTO THE AREA, AND THEN FIGHT OVER WHO GETS TO DATE HER?

23. WHAT IS THE NAME OF MONICA AND ROSS' COUSIN THAT STAYS WITH CHANDLER AND MONICA, AND THEN ROSS?

24. WHICH CELEBRITY ACTORS FEATURES IN 'THE ONE WITH MONICA'S AND CHANDLER'S WEDDING'?

25. WHAT DOES TAG GET RACHEL FOR HER 30TH BIRTHDAY?

26. WHAT INSTRUMENT DOES ROSS WANT TO PLAY AT MONICA AND CHANDLER'S WEDDING?

Hard

27. What apartment number is Monica's?

28. What did Rachel do to 'steal Monica's thunder' at her sixteenth birthday party?

29. Why did Rachel's father buy her a boat when she was 15?

30. What phrase does Rachel say to Joey when sailing that makes her realise that she is like her father?

31. Where was Phoebe's grandmother's secret cookie recipe actually from?

32. When Joey is offered to come back onto 'Days of Our Lives', what is the name of the character he is offered to play?

33. What is Phoebe's response when Rachel says, 'I just wanna apologise. I'm really sorry I was a baby'?

34. In 'The One with All the Cheesecakes', where was the cheesecake from?

35. What did Ross buy when he turned 30?

36. Joey is a part Portuguese, how much?

37. JOEY AND ROSS ARE DECIDING ON A SPENDING LIMIT FOR WHEN THEY EACH TAKE OUT CHRISTEN. HOW MUCH DOES JOEY SUGGEST?

38. WHAT TYPE OF AWARD IS JOEY NOMINATED FOR FOR HIS ROLE IN DAYS OF OUR LIVES?

39. TO WHAT SONG DO MONICA AND CHANDLER GET MARRIED?

40. WHEN CHANDLER AND ROSS EACH GET CELEBRITY'S TUXEDOS TO WEAR TO CHANDLER AND MONICA'S WEDDING, WHOSE DO THEY CHOOSE?

SEASON 7 ANSWERS

EASY

1. TAG.

2. HANUKKAH.

3. TRUE.

4. ROSS AND JOEY.

5. RACHEL.

6. HE SAYS THAT HE LOVES HIM.

7. ROSS.

8. HE WAS APPLYING TO BE HER ASSISTANT AT WORK

9. SHE IS TRYING TO MAKE RACHEL WANT TO STOP LIVING WITH HIM.

10. AS HIS 'JOEY'S APPLE'

MEDIUM

11. THEY KISS.

12. PHOEBE'S.

13. HE ONCE KISSED A GUY.

14. THE HOLIDAY ARMADILLO.

15. CHEESECAKE.

16. JOEY.

17. BELARUS.

18. SHE PUTS IT DOWN THE TRASH CHUTE.

19. TAG.

20. CHANDLER'S FAMILY IS PART SCOTTISH.

21. CHANDLER: 'STAYING OUT OF THE WAY'.

22. CHRISTEN.

23. CASSIE.

24. GARY OLDMAN.

25. A SCOOTER

26. THE BAGPIPES.

HARD

27. 20.

28. SHE WENT TO THIRD BASE WITH MONICA'S COUSIN, CHARLIE.

29. HER PONY WAS SICK.

30. 'GREEN'S DON'T QUIT'.

31. NESTLE TOLL HOUSE.

32. DR STRYKER RAMORAY.

33. 'THAT'S RIDICULOUS, RACHEL, WE WERE ALL BABIES ONCE'.

34. MAMAS LITTLE BAKERY.

35. A RED SPORTS CAR.

36. ONE SIXTEENTH.

37. $6.

38. A 'SOAPIE'.

39. EVERLONG, BY THE FOO FIGHTERS.

40. JAMES BOND'S AND BATMAN'S, RESPECTIVELY.

Season 8 Questions

Easy

1. When Rachel and Ross are disagreeing about who came onto whom, and they watch the video back to determine it, who had come onto whom?

2. Who came up with the story about backpacking across Europe?

3. Whose did the red sweater that was used to work out who the father to Rachel's baby was belong to?

4. Who wins the arm wrestle between Ross and Chandler?

5. Which of the gang does Will Colbert (Brad Pitt) not like?

6. What happens to Chandler's hand after he plays Ms Pac-Man all day?

7. When Monica get Chandler to have a bath, what does she give him to make it a 'boy bath'?

MEDIUM

8. WHAT CLUB DID WILL COLBERT (BRAD PITT) HAVE WITH ROSS AT HIGH SCHOOL.

9. WHEN MONICA EXPLAINS THAT SHE IS NOT PREGNANT IN THE OPENING EPISODE OF SERIES 8, WHO CLAIMS THEY ARE INSTEAD?

10. WHERE DO ROSS AND MONA MEET?

11. WHAT IS CHANDLER'S MIDDLE NAME?

12. ONE OF CHANDLER'S COLLEAGUES THINKS HIS NAME IS SOMETHING OTHER THAN CHANDLER. WHAT IS IT?

13. WHAT IS URSULA'S FIANCE CALLED?

14. WHY IS MONICA SUSPICIOUS OF THE MAID THEY GET?

15. WHICH FAMOUS ACTOR COMES TO THANKSGIVING IN SERIES 8?

16. WHAT CHALLENGE DOES JOEY HAVE AT THANKSGIVING?

17. WHICH ONE OF JOEY'S SISTERS IS PREGNANT?

18. WHEN MONA ASKS ROSS WHERE THEIR RELATIONSHIP IS GOING, WHAT DOES HE DO?

19. WHAT GAME DOES PHOEBE GIVE TO MONICA AND CHANDLER AS A PRESENT?

20. WHAT DOES RACHEL TELL JOEY IS HER BIG WORK PROBLEM, BECAUSE THINGS ARE AWKWARD BETWEEN THE TWO OF THEM?

21. WHICH KNOWN CHARACTER IS IN THE SAME MATERNITY WARD AS RACHEL?

22. WHAT IS THE BIG SHOCK AT THE END OF THE SERIES?

Hard

23. When Phoebe is telling Monica, Chandler, and Rachel at the wedding that she is pregnant, who does she claim is the father?

24. What size are Joey's feet?

25. What is the name of the couple that Monica and Chandler meet on their honeymoon?

26. What fake name does Joey use?

27. What fake name does Phoebe use?

28. When Monica and Chandler host a fancy dress Halloween party, how does Rachel describe what she came as?

29. At the same Halloween party, what does Monica come as?

30. At the same party, what does Joey dress up as?

31. At the same party, what does Ross dress up as?

32. At the same party, what does Chandler dress up as?

33. AT THE SAME PARTY, WHAT DOES PHOEBE DRESS UP AS?

34. WHAT IS RACHEL'S MIDDLE NAME?

35. WHERE DID RACHEL GROW UP?

36. WHAT IS PHOEBE'S RENDITION OF ROXANNE BY THE POLICE, WHEN SHE WANTS ROSS TO GET TICKETS FROM STING.

37. WHERE DID JOEY GROW UP?

38. WHAT ARE PHOEBE'S SUGGESTIONS FOR ROSS AND RACHEL'S BABY?

39. ACCORDING TO JOEY, HOW WAS HE DESCRIBED IN HIS FIRST 'GOOD' REVIEW?

40. WHAT DOES JOEY SUSPECT IS HIDDEN IN MONICA'S SECRET CLOSET?

Season 8 Answers

Easy

1. Rachel came onto Ross.

2. Joey.

3. Ross.

4. Chandler lets Ross win.

5. Rachel.

6. It becomes claw shaped.

7. A toy boat.

Medium

8. The 'I Hate Rachel Green Club'.

9. Phoebe.

10. Monica and Chandler's wedding.

11. Muriel.

12. Toby.

13. Eric.

14. She thinks she is stealing her clothes.

15. Brad Pitt.

16. To eat the entire turkey.

17. Dina.

18. He gives her a key to his house.

19. Ms Pac-Man.

20. She says her boss wants to buy her baby.

21. Janis.

22. Joey (accidentally) proposes to Rachel.

Hard

23. James Brolin.

24. 7.

25. Greg and Ginny.

26. Ken Adams.

27. Regina Phalange.

28. A woman, who spent a lot of money

ON A DRESS, AND SHE WANTS TO WEAR IT BECAUSE SOON SHE WON'T BE ABLE TO FIT INTO IT.

29. CAT WOMAN.

30. CHANDLER.

31. SPUDNIK.

32. A PINK BUNNY.

33. SUPER GIRL.

34. KAREN.

35. LONG ISLAND.

36. 'ROSS CAN'.

37. QUEENS.

38. FOR A GIRL, PHOEBE. FOR A BOY, PHOEBO.

39. 'JOEY TRIBBIANI WAS ABISMAL'.

40. RICHARD.

SEASON 9 QUESTIONS

EASY

1. WHO WALKS IN DURING JOEY'S PROPOSAL TO RACHEL?

2. WHAT DO ROSS AND RACHEL CALL THEIR BABY?

3. SHOULD RACHEL AND ROSS DIE, WHO DO THEY SAY WOULD TAKE CARE OF EMMA?

4. WHAT SONG ON THE RECORDER DOES SANDY TEACH JOEY??

5. WHAT DOES PHOEBE SAY WHEN MIKE PROPOSES IN BARBADOS?

6. WHEN THE GANG GO TO BUY LOTTERY TICKETS, WHO DOESN'T INITIALLY WANT TO BUY ANY?

7. TRUE OR FALSE? THE GANG WIN THE LOTTERY JACKPOT.

8. WHAT IS THE NAME OF THE NEW PALEONTOLOGIST TO ROSS' DEPARTMENT?

9. WHO DOES JOEY KISS AT HIS ROOFTOP PARTY?

10. TRUE OR FALSE, PHOEBE NEVER TELLS MIKE THAT VIKRUM WAS MADE UP?

Q11. WHY DOESN'T ROSS LIKE THEIR NEW NANNY, SANDY?

MEDIUM

12. WHAT DO THE GROUP BUY RACHEL AFTER SHE GIVES BIRTH TO EMMA?

13. WHEN CHANDLER FALLS ASLEEP IN A WORK MEETING, WHERE DOES HE ACCIDENTALLY AGREE TO MOVE TO TO WORK?

14. WHAT DOES JOEY WANT ROSS TO DO TO MAKE HIM FEEL BETTER ABOUT JOEY PROPOSING TO RACHEL?

15. WHAT DOES JOEY WRITE AS ROSS' OCCUPATION ON THE HOSPITAL FORM?

16. WHEN ROSS AND RACHEL HIRE A MALE NANNY, WHAT QUIP DOES CHANDLER MAKE?

17. WHAT SONG DOES ROSS SING TO EMMA TO MAKE HER LAUGH?

18. WHEN PHOEBE MUGGED ROSS WHEN THEY WERE YOUNGER, WHAT COMIC OF HIS DID SHE STEAL?

19. WHEN MIKE PROPOSES TO PHOEBE IN BARBADOS, AND SHE SAYS NO, WHAT IS DAVID'S NEXT LINE?

20. WHEN THE GANG GO TO BUY LOTTERY TICKETS, HOW MUCH IS SUGGESTED THAT THEY EACH PUT IN?

21. HOW DOES PHOEBE LOSE THE LOTTERY TICKETS THAT THEY ALL CHIP IN TO BUY?

22. When Monica can't go away with Chandler to Vermont, who does he take instead?

23. What is the name of the imaginary boyfriend that Ross tells Mike that Phoebe had?

24. Why were Ross and Rachel late to Phoebe's birthday dinner?

25. Ross, Rachel, Chandler and Monica were all late to Phoebe's birthday dinner, but who were the last there?

26. Which ex-boyfriend comes back into Phoebe's life as she's seeing Mike?

27. What is the name of the nanny that Rachel and Ross hire?

28. What's the one kind of boat that can never ever sink?

HARD

29. WHEN TRYING TO CONVINCE MONICA TO MOVE, WHAT DOES CHANDLER DESCRIBE TULSA AS?

30. WHAT DID PHOEBE SAY TO ROSS YEARS AGO WHEN SHE WAS MUGGING HIM?

31. WHAT IS EMMA'S FIRST WORD?

32. WHICH TV ADVERT HAS A MONKEY IN IT, WHICH MAKES ROSS NOSTALGIC ABOUT MARCEL?

33. WHEN THE GANG DECIDE TO SHARE A LOAD OF LOTTERY TICKETS, WHO BUYS MORE WITHOUT THE OTHERS KNOWING?

34. AFTER PHOEBE DROPS THE GANGS LOTTERY TICKETS OFF THE BALCONY, THE GANG SEARCH FOR THEM AND RETURN TO TWO TELEPHONE MESSAGES. WHO ARE THEY FROM, AND WHAT DO THEY SAY?

35. WHEN THE GANG PLAY THE LOTTERY, HOW MUCH DO THEY WIN?

36. WHY DOES JOEY GET THE GANG TICKETS TO A PLAY THAT HE SAYS HE CAN'T GO TO HIMSELF BECAUSE HE HAS WORK?

37. WHEN PHOEBE GIVES RACHEL A MASSAGE AT THE BIG CORPORATION, AND TRIES TO PRETEND IT ISN'T HER, WHAT DOES SHE SAY HER NAME IS?

38. WHY WAS PHOEBE CRYING, WHEN SHE WAS TALKING TO ROSS IN CENTRAL PERK, BEFORE HER DATE WITH MIKE?

39. WHEN CHANDLER COMES BACK FROM TULSA, HOW MUCH HAD HE SMOKED IN THE TWO DAYS HE WAS THERE?

40. WHICH NEW COLLEAGUE OF MONICA'S MAKES CHANDLER JEALOUS BECAUSE HE'S 'WITHOUT A DOUBT THE FUNNIEST GUY' SHE'S EVER MET?

SEASON 9 ANSWERS

EASY

1. ROSS.

2. EMMA.

3. MONICA AND CHANDLER

4. HOT CROSS BUNS.

5. 'NO'.

6. ROSS.

7. FALSE.

8. CHARLIE.

9. CHARLIE.

10. FALSE.

11. HE SAYS HE INS'T MANLY ENOUGH.

MEDIUM

12. A GIANT STUFFED GORILLA.

13. TULSA, OKLAHOMA.

14. HIT HIM.

15. DINOSAURS.

16. 'YOU HIRED A MANNY?'

17. 'BABY GOT BACK'.

18. SCIENCE BOY.

19. 'HAHA'.

20. $50.

21. A PIGEON FLIES INTO HER AND SHE DROPS THEM OFF THE BALCONY.

22. ROSS.

23. VIKRUM.

24. THEY GOT LOCKED OUT OF THE APARTMENT WITH EMMA IN.

25. CHANDLER AND MONICA.

26. DAVID.

27. SANDY.

28. A FRIEND-SHIP.

HARD

29. THE PARIS OF OKLAHOMA.

30. 'GIVE ME YOUR MONEY, PUNK'.

31. 'GLEBA'.

32. MONKEY.

33. MONICA.

34. THE FIRST IS PHOEBE IMPERSONATING THE PIGEON THAT KNOCKED THE TICKETS OFF HER, APOLOGISING. THE SECOND IS FROM A MAN CALLED CHARLIE, INFORMING CHANDLER THAT HE DID NOT GET THE JOB HE APPLIED FOR.

35. $3.

36. BECAUSE HE IS HOSTING A PARTY FOR THE CAST FROM DAYS OF OUR LIVES.

37. IKEA.

38. SHE REALISED THAT SHE'D NEVER HAD A LONG TERM RELATIONSHIP.

39. THREE CARTONS.

40. JEFFREY.

Season 10 Questions

Easy

1. When Chandler and Monica visit Phoebe's friends that have an adopted child, what mistake does Chandler make?

2. How does Ross find out about Joey and Rachel?

3. What condition does Chandler give to Monica to untie her when her hair is stuck to the shower curtain?

4. What problem does Ross have when he goes to get a spray on tan?

5. What does Amy do that upsets Ross and Rachel when she takes Emma out for the day?

6. How does Phoebe propose to Mike?

7. Which two ways did Mike plan to propose to Phoebe?

8. True or false, Emma wins at the beauty pageant?

9. What important news do Monica and Chandler find out at Thanksgiving?

10. WHAT IS THE NAME OF THE WOMAN WHOSE CHILD MONICA AND ROSS IS ADOPTING?

MEDIUM

11. WHAT FOOD DOES ROSS MAKE DURING THE DOUBLE DATE BETWEEN ROSS AND CHARLIE, AND JOEY AND RACHEL?

12. WHAT DRINKS DOES ROSS MAKE DURING THE DOUBLE DATE BETWEEN ROSS AND CHARLIE, AND JOEY AND RACHEL?

13. WHAT IS THE NAME OF MONICA'S AND PHOEBE'S OLD FRIEND THAT MOVED BACK FROM ENGLAND?

14. WHAT PRESENT DOES JOEY GET FOR EMMA'S FIRST BIRTHDAY?

15. WHAT PRESENT DOES PHOEBE GET FOR EMMA'S FIRST BIRTHDAY?

16. HOW DO MONICA, CHANDLER, JOEY AND PHOEBE DECIDE WHO GETS TO LEAVE EMMA'S BIRTHDAY PARTY?

17. WHAT DOES AMY DECIDE SHE IS GOING TO HAVE A CAREER IN?

18. HOW DOES JOEY KNOW CHANDLER DIDN'T WATCH THE TAPE WITH HIS ACTING ON IT?

19. WHY WERE JOEY AND ROSS LATE TO MONICA'S AND CHANDLER'S FOR THANKSGIVING?

20. WHY WERE RACHEL AND PHOEBE LATE TO MONICA AND CHANDLER'S THANKSGIVING?

21. WHEN THE GANG PLAY ROCK, PAPER, SCISSORS TO DECIDE WHO MUST GO INTO MONICA'S AND CHANDLER'S FOR THANKSGIVING FIRST, WHAT MOVE DOES JOEY PLAY?

22. WHEN THE GANG PLAY ROCK, PAPER, SCISSORS TO DECIDE WHO MUST GO INTO MONICA'S AND CHANDLER'S FOR THANKSGIVING FIRST, WHAT MOVE DOES PHOEBE PLAY?

23. WHAT DOES CHANDLER JOKINGLY NAME HIS CRANBERRY SAUCE?

24. WHEN JOEY'S HEAD GETS STUCK IN THE DOOR AT THANKSGIVING, HOW DO THEY TRY FIRST TRY TO GET HIM OUT?

HARD

25. WHAT DO WE LEARN ABOUT CHARLIE'S FATHER DURING THE DOUBLE DATE BETWEEN ROSS AND CHARLIE, AND JOEY AND RACHEL?

26. WHY DOES FRANK J.R NOT WANT TO GIVE CHANDLER TO PHOEBE?

27. WHY DOES FRANK J.R NOT WANT TO GIVE FRANK JR JR TO PHOEBE?

28. WHY DOES FRANK J.R NOT WANT TO GIVE LESLIE TO PHOEBE?

29. WHAT JOKE DOES DOES FRANK J.R J.R COME UP WITH THAT IMPRESSES HIS FATHER?

30. WHAT DOES CHANDLER OFFER OWEN IN EXCHANGE FOR NOT TELLING HIS PARENTS THAT HE TOLD HIM HE'S ADOPTED?

- DURING THE DOUBLE DATE BETWEEN ROSS AND CHARLIE, AND JOEY AND RACHEL, ROSS ASSIGNS A MEANING TO EACH OF THE LETTERS THAT SPELL LOVE. WHAT ARE THEY?

31.
32.
33.
34.

35. After the double date between Ross and Charlie, and Joey and Rachel, when does he take off his pants (trousers) and shoes?

36. What plans did Chandler and Monica have on Emma's birthday?

37. What does Amy think Ross does for a living?

38. What of Phoebe's does she try to give to either Monica or Rachel, because Mike doesn't want her to keep it?

39. How much does Emma win at the beauty pageant?

40. What does Chandler make for the Thanksgiving dinner?

41. When Monica and Chandler are told they're going to adopt a baby, where is the mother from?

42. What does Emma wear to the beauty pageant.

43. Which character from 'Parks and Recreation' cameos in episode 9, The One with the Birth Mother?

SEASON 10 ANSWERS

EASY

1. HE TELLS THE CHILD HE IS ADOPTED

2. HE WALKS IN ON THEM KISSING.

3. THAT SHE MAKES HER HAIR NORMAL AGAIN.

4. HE SPRAYS HIS FRONT FOUR TIMES, MAKING HIS FRONT AN '8', AND HIS BACK A '0'.

5. SHE PIERCES EMMA'S EARS

6. AT A KNICKS GAME.

7. FIRST AT A KNICKS GAME, AND THEN HE HIDES THE RING IN HER CAKE.

8. TRUE.

9. THE THEY'RE ABLE TO ADOPT A BABY.

10. ERICA.

MEDIUM

11. FAJITAS.

12. MARGARITAS.

13. AMANDA.

14. HE DOES A DRAMATIC READING OF ONE OF HER BOOKS.

15. SHE PERFORMS HER A SONG.

16. THEY HAVE A RACE BETWEEN THREE TOYS.

17. AS A BABY STYLIST.

18. BECAUSE THERE WAS AN EMBARRASSING TAPE ON IT, AND HE WOULD'VE MADE A COMMENT.

19. THEY WERE AT AN ICE HOCKEY GAME.

20. THEY TOOK EMMA TO A BEAUTY PAGEANT.

21. FIRE.

22. WATER BALLOON.

23. CHANBERRY SAUCE.

24. They put turkey grease on his head.

Hard

25. He is a raging alcoholic.

26. She is the smartest of the triplets.

27. He is the funniest

28. She can burp the alphabet.

29. What's green and says hey, I'm a frog?
A talking frog.

30. $50.

31. L = Is for love, for what is life, without love?

32. O = Is for oh wow!

33. V = For this very surprising turn of events.

34. E = How extremely normal he finds it.

35. When he was dancing to the Chicago soundtrack.

36. A weekend away in Vermont.

37. That he owns a falafel cart.

38. A painting she made, called Gladys.

39. $1000 dollars.

40. Cranberry sauce.

41. Ohio..

42. An Alicia Mae Emery costume.

43. Jerry.

Printed in Great Britain
by Amazon

63513543R00050